Wheels, Wings, and Water

Bicycles

Lola M. Schaefer

Heinemann Library
Chicago, Illinois

Customer Service 888-454-2279
Visit our website at www.heinemannlibrary.com

Designed by Sue Emerson, Heinemann Library; Page layout by Que-Net Media
Printed and bound in the United States by Lake Book Manufacturing, Inc.
Photo research by Amor Montes De Oca

07 06 05 04 03
10 9 8 7 6 5 4 3 2 1

Library of Congress Cataloging-in-Publication Data
Schaefer, Lola M., 1950-
  Bicycles / Lola M. Schaefer.
       v. cm. – (Wheels, wings, and water)
Includes index.
Contents: What are bicycles? – What do bicycles look like? – What are bicycles made of? – How did bicycles look long ago? – What is a BMX bike? – What is a racing bike? – What is a track bike? – What is a mountain bike? – What are some special bikes? – Quiz – Picture glossary.
  ISBN 1-4034-0878-5 (HC), 1-4034-3617-7 (Pbk.)
  1. Bicycles–Juvenile literature. [1. Bicycles.] I. Title. II. Series.
  TL412.S33 2003
  629.227'2–dc21

                                2002014720

Acknowledgments
The author and publishers are grateful to the following for permission to reproduce copyright material:
p. 4 Larry Williams and Associates/Corbis; p. 5 Jean-Yves Ruszniewski/Corbis; pp. 6, 15 David Madison/Bruce Coleman, Inc.; p. 7 Spencer Grant/PhotoEdit, Inc.; p. 8 Philip Gould/Corbis; p. 9 Gary W. Carter; p. 10 Hulton-Deutsch Collection/Corbis; p. 11 Bettmann/Corbis; p. 12 Tony Freeman/PhotoEdit, Inc.; p. 13 Jane Faircloth/Transparencies, Inc.; pp. 14, 18, 22, 24 PhotoDisc/Getty Images; p. 16 William Cornett/Image Excellence Communications; p. 17 Matthew Stockman/AllSport/Getty Images; p. 19 Donnelle Oxley; p. 20 David Madison Sports Images, Inc.; p. 21 Kevin R. Morris/Corbis; p. 23 row 1 (L-R) Jane Faircloth/Transparencies, Inc., Philip Gould/Corbis; row 2 (L-R) PhotoDisc/Getty Images; Kevin R. Morris/Corbis; PhotoDisc/Getty Images; row 3 (L-R) Gary W. Carter; David Madison Sports Images, Inc.; Matthew Stockman/AllSport/Getty Images; row 4 David Madison/Bruce Coleman, Inc.; back cover PhotoDisc/Getty Images

Cover photograph by Stephen Welstead/Corbis

Every effort has been made to contact copyright holders of any material reproduced in this book. Any omissions will be rectified in subsequent printings if notice is given to the publisher.

Special thanks to our advisory panel for their help in the preparation of this book:

Alice Bethke, Library Consultant
Palo Alto, CA

Eileen Day, Preschool Teacher
Chicago, IL

Kathleen Gilbert,
Second Grade Teacher
Round Rock, TX

Sandra Gilbert,
Library Media Specialist
Fiest Elementary School
Houston, TX

Jan Gobeille,
Kindergarten Teacher
Garfield Elementary
Oakland, CA

Angela Leeper,
Educational Consultant
North Carolina Department
of Public Instruction
Wake Forest, NC

Some words are shown in bold, **like this.**
You can find them in the picture glossary on page 23.

Contents

What Are Bicycles?

Bicycles are **vehicles** with two wheels.

Bicycles can carry people and things.

brake

pedal

People push **pedals** to make bicycles move.

They use brakes to stop.

What Do Bicycles Look Like?

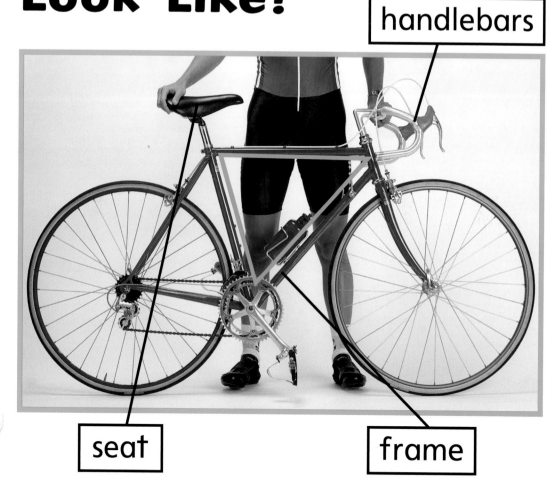

handlebars

seat

frame

Bicycle **frames** look like **triangles.**

Bicycles have seats and **handlebars.**

They have two **pedals,** too.

Bicycles can be many colors.

What Are Bicycles Made Of?

frame

pedal

Bicycle **frames** are made of metal.

Some **pedals** are made of metal and rubber.

seat

handgrips

tire

Tires and **handgrips** are made of rubber.

Bicycle seats are made of plastic.

How Did Bicycles Look Long Ago?

The first bicycles were made of wood.

Riders pushed them with their feet.

Later, bicycles had **pedals.**

They had big front wheels and little back wheels.

What Is a BMX Bicycle?

BMX bicycles are small and light.

BMX means "bicycle motorcross."

People ride BMX bicycles on
dirt tracks.

Some people call BMX bicycles
dirt bikes.

What Is a Racing Bicycle?

Racing bicycles are very light.

They go fast in races.

Riders lean low over the **handlebars.**

They have to push the **pedals** hard to go fast.

What Is a Track Bicycle?

Track bicycles and racing bikes look alike.

But track bikes do not have brakes.

People ride track bikes in
a **velodrome**.

They pedal very fast to stay up
on the steep sides.

What Is a Mountain Bicycle?

tire

Mountain bikes have thick, bumpy tires.

These can roll over sticks and rocks.

People ride mountain bikes on trails.

Some people ride mountain bikes up hills.

What Are Some Special Bicycles?

Tandems are bicycles for two people.

They have two seats and two sets of **handlebars.**

Pedicabs have three wheels.

People can ride in a pedicab.

Quiz

Do you know what kind of bicycle this is?

Can you find it in the book?

Look for the answer on page 24.

Picture Glossary

dirt track
page 13

pedal
pages 5, 7, 8, 11, 15

triangle
page 6

frame
pages 6, 8

pedicab
page 21

vehicle
page 4

handgrips
page 9

tandem
page 20

velodrome
page 17

handlebars
pages 6, 15, 20

Note to Parents and Teachers

Reading for information is an important part of a child's literacy development. Learning begins with a question about something. Help children think of themselves as investigators and researchers by encouraging their questions about the world around them. Each chapter in this book begins with a question. Read the question together. Talk about what you think the answer might be. Read the text to find out if your predictions were correct. Think of other questions you could ask about the topic, and discuss where you might find the answers. In this book, the picture glossary symbol for vehicle is a bicycle. Explain to children that a vehicle is something that can move people or things from one place to another. Some vehicles have motors, like cars, but others do not.

Index

Answer to quiz on page 22
This is a mountain bike.